Eddy

Noreen Lace

Introduction:

Eddy is a fictional and imaginative rendering of an actual event in Poe's life.

In November 1848, Edgar Allan Poe ingested a near-fatal overdose of laudanum. It is unclear whether this was accidental or purposeful. While some blame an addiction to drugs and alcohol as leading to this overdose, others call attention to his wife's death a year earlier and rumors of prolonged depression.

This overdose took place four days prior to the famous picture for which he is well recognized and is unrelated to his actual death, eleven months later, on the seventh of October in 1849.

Laudanum is a mixture of opium and alkaloids of morphine and codeine. It was readily available at any number of pharmacies, markets, and even confectionaries. Although the suggested use was for headaches or other illnesses, it was used for all sorts of reasons and, as we understand today, it is highly addictive.

In the last months of Edgar Allan Poe's life, he moved back to Richmond, courted Elmira Royster Shelton (among other women), and joined The Sons of the Temperance Movement, an organization which worked toward abstinence and the prohibition of alcohol.

A modern test of his hair shaft showed insignificant alcohol or drug use in his last months of life.

Noreen Lace

For my daughters
who've changed a gray abstract idea of
love into the tangible beauty of life.

.

He stumbles from the pub, slips, and falls on the iced over bricks of Boston's November streets. Save for the muddled voices beyond the closed door, the street is quiet as his body thuds to the ground. His breath billows in front of him as he gasps and grumbles and struggles to his knees, then his feet, to regain his drunken balance.

The gaslamp on the corner offers a wavering yellow glow for the struggling figure on the lonely winter night. Thin strands of hair blow in the chilled breeze; he runs his hands over his head, straightens himself before he pulls at the sagging overcoat and tugs it closed.

Remembering the tinctures of laudanum pried from the chary pharmacist, he hurriedly shoves his hands in his pockets, retrieves the bottles.

His heavy breath mounds in front of him and, for a moment, he can't see; then the luminous cloud of brandy scented air dissipates. The medicines are intact. Relieved, he stuffs them back in his pocket and buttons his jacket.

"Edgar," someone calls from the corner; the noise from the pub trails the swarthy figure out until the door slams to a close behind him. "You alright?"

Edgar waves him off without turning around.

The thick shadow chuckles as he staggers in the opposite direction.

The winter is freezing cold, but the snow hasn't endured. Small white crystals pile in corners and fill the air. The icy rain soaks him before he reaches his chamber on the second floor of the boarding house. The room is small, impersonal, but warmer than the street. An unlit lantern shimmies on the desk as he unsteadily seats himself, glances out the window.

A barely discernable outline disquiets the otherwise muted darkness on the corner of the street below. He knows it's the black dog that's stalked him his whole life. Suddenly angered, he shoves himself forward, pushes the unlit lamp aside and topples the ink jar.

"Get outta here, you wretched creature." The incensed command lost in the night.

Recovering the secreted bottles of opium from his coat pocket, he sets them side by side in front of him. Unsteadily he tugs the lid from one and snorts in a single gulp.

The tonic soothes his racing mind, slows the raging blood. He leans back in the chair, allows his fingers to linger on the beaten old wood of the writing table. The puddled black ink pools before it tendrils out in spidery veins. As his breath smooths to a measured plodding, the black ink recasts to red. The splatters of bright red blood spatters on the sweat soaked sheets of his mother, the sprays of crimson on the tender white fingers of his wife as she play the ivory keys of the piano.

He pushes his fingers through the mire. The blood and blackness race up his arm, overtake him, swallow him; inside a cask, a coffin, he is buried. He claws and kicks at the wood before he hears the sweet harmony of his mother's voice.

"Eddy. Eddy honey." Her voice is music and laughter; the melody courses through his body alongside the drug, stirs each blood cell, excites every nerve ending until he feels more alive than he's ever felt.

The clack of heeled shoes on the wooden floor, tin make-up compacts clink on the vanity, hand held mirrors clap the dressing tables. The once familiar hustle of the backstage theater work their way into his sodden brain.

She's with him. He's a child held on her small warm lap with her gentle arms around him. Her soft pink lips brush the back of his head. He feels warm and loved and protected.

A boy of two, he watches his mother pat rouge on her dove-like skin. She's hot, too. A boiler around him. Her hard won breath is sour with sickness. She coughs and sets him down. His shoes snap on the old oak floorboards. He waits. The rising thunder of the theater goers filters back as a man calls out, too loud, "Five minutes."

The ladies help his petite mother into her costume, fasten it. Near barking, she tries to push the rasp from her throat before the play begins. She wipes her mouth; the familiar ruby splash left on the cloth lay on the dressing table in front of him. The rouge fades into her sallow skin, she applies more, then tints her lips.

"Be a good boy for momma, watch Rosalie." She leans down and kisses his forehead; her fevered lips burn his skin. Her eyes sparkle with the glow of joyful angels, but the ashen irises betray a lost and frightened soul in the mist.

She is always like this, for as long as he remembers; her snowy skin, her pallid eyes, the tint of rose always about her mouth.

Somewhere, somehow, there is always the trace of red.

He glances at the small wooden cradle where the baby sleeps before following his mother to the stage door.

The lights are low. The great breaths and small whispers of the audience's anticipation fills the Richmond Theater. This is his favorite moment: The dimmed hall, the baited snuffle of anticipation, and the indistinct outlines of the actors in place. Then the gas-lamps pop, voices vibrate; the reanimation of life as the spectators focus on his mother.

He has spent his young life here, half in the shadows, observing one play or another from side stage. It's an odd view. People speak to one another for an audience he rarely glimpses, but they never speak to him, never look at him. He is a lone voyeur, invisible to all, until he catches the wink of his mother's eye just before she turns away.

The excitement of passion fills the stage and words float through the air. They mingle in storm like fashion and drain down the stairs in front of him. He steps back, mesmerized by the spectacle.

When it's over, the laughter, tears, exhales, the applause, always the applause. The overflow of emotions from the audience brought on by the actors; it's a sweet allocation of control by performer to viewer.

They bow; his mother nearly falters before two of her co-stars catch her, hold her. They bend again, the curtain descends, and she returns to him.

Tonight, they help her off stage and into the chair in front of her old gilt mirror.

"She's still asleep, Elizabeth." One of the actresses checks on Rosalie. "She's such a quiet baby."

"Hardly ever cries." His mother's voice is soft and low, hides the strain.

In the midnight, the baby in one arm, Edgar's hand in the other, she walks though the near empty streets of Virginia's autumn; the trees, lit with the bright fire of colors during the day turn beige and brown in the bleak night. The little family fights against the early cold spell, up the two flights of stairs, to their tiny room above the city.

The air is more chilled inside than out. His mother lies down. Her cough comes in sanguine spurts, not like the tinted lipstick or the rouge that colors her cheeks, but bright like the lingering rays of sunset on an autumn evening, just before it all turns brown and stains the earth, stains the sheets.

"Come here." The serene chime of her whispers caress him. "My bonny little boy." Her hot touch sears his skin as she urges him in the bed next to her. The fire of her body warms him on the brisk October night.

Just before her gasps wane, before he cascades into a slumber, Edgar recognizes the first rays of daylight as they stretch into the horizon to trace the ebony night.

"Eddy, no." Her murmur dissolves into the rain pulsing the window.

"Mother," he whispers as he raises his head, reaches his blood covered hand out in front of him.

He smashes his fist down on the desk. The ink stains his fingers as he claws the wood, tries to scratch his way out of the dream.

"Mother," he whispers again with finality.

His eyes adjust to the cimmerian room as he searches for the opium that will, if not bring his mother back to him, take him to her. He wrenches the corked top and gulps. Life be damned.

His heart pounds so hard his chest seems to crack. He gulps in air, swallows spit, and… he thinks he tastes blood.

He tries to catch his breath, certain his lungs will burst even as his head explodes with thoughts, stories, memories. He squeezes his eyes close, squints them open and gasps.

It's a bright-hot early-fall day and Edgar's running as if his life depends on it. He slows and stops after the finish line, doubling over the faint white chalk in the dirt. He's won.

Sweat forms on his brow, drips from his temples as his competitor catches up with him.

"Eddy, damn it. How do you do it?" The
young man slaps his back. "You win at everything,
footraces, swimming, and the girls." Rob nudges at
his companion's shoulder as a few of their female
classmates pass.

Edgar stands straight, taller than his
classmate, and smiles at the young women, then
takes a jab at his friend and shakes his head. He's
not interested and, even if he were, the young
lady's father would find reason to object. He's been
through this before; he may live in the house of one
of Virginia's most well-respected men, but he's still
the son of an actress. Low born, he's heard them
say.

"Let's go. My mother's waiting." Rob pokes
his hand at Edgar.

At the Stanard house, he is a welcomed
friend. The two story residence sits on the corner,
not far from the school, and it's a happy pause
before Edgar returns home. Rob's father is rarely
present, but his mother dotes on the boys, scurries
the servants for snacks, drinks, dinner. Then she
sits with them until they tire of her. But Edgar
never wearies of her, and he comes sometimes
more for her now than his classmate.

"Have you brought me any poetry." Her
voice is silken and round. It fills the empty space in
his soul. He studies her across the room, soft curls
around her slim face, and the smile always dancing
in her eyes. She is perfect, Edgar thinks. Rob is a
lucky man.

"I have," he says, but he doesn't reach yet to
retrieve it. He waits for her to say so, doesn't wish
to appear presumptuous.

"Let's go into the parlor then. You can read to us." She pauses a moment before turning out of the room.

"This is where I beg off." Rob calls behind her. "You and your poetry. I'll leave you to it. Come find me when you're done." He puts his hand on Edgar's shoulder, gives him a playful nudge.

Mrs. Stanard listens as he reads quietly but confidently. He wants no one to hear but her, not that he'd be embarrassed but because all of this is for her now.

They sit in front of the barren fireplace. They have not yet brought in the wood for the start of the cool evenings. The swirled marble and the pearl tile add lightness to the room. The linens are white, the settee is alabaster, as are the pillows and the chairs in which they sit. It might be harsh to some, but it is the fair glow of this room that soothes the sharp edges of the world around him.

Here he is not an orphan, not low born. Here he is valued. And she is the luminescence that warms his heart, gives him the motivation to go on.

When he finishes the last poem, she sits forward and reaches for his hand. "Edgar, those are beautiful. You have true talent."

She is a woman of the world. The wife of a powerful attorney and judge. She is the kindest soul in the world. And he trusts her. They talk for hours about poetry, before dusk calls, before Rob reenters the room, before he starts for home in the first chill of autumn.

Rob doesn't attend classes, the house is closed up, and the servants do not let Edgar in. He comes late one night through the sleeting rain to feign interest in Rob's health. He is concerned about his absent friend, but he's heard his own adoptive mother whisper that the lady of the house has taken ill, not the son. The valet stops him at the door.

"I tell you, I must see Robert," Eddy insists.

It's not Robert who appears in the foyer, but his father. A man Edgar has met only once. He's a busy man with no time for pleasantries, no time for the lovely wife he neglects. Although Edgar shows him the respect a man in his position deserves, he does not like him.

"Is Robert well?" Eddy asks.

Mr. Stanard nods his head. "Well enough."

"And your wife, Mrs. Stanard, is she well?"

Mr. Stanard nods his head at the young man. He may or may not have heard mention of this particular schoolmate. Other things flood his mind at the moment; he looks distracted.

"I'm Edgar Poe." He holds out his hand. "I've read my poetry to your family, which I think they've quite enjoyed. I'm friends with..." Eddy thinks it would be imprudent to say he is friends with the man's wife; the lie itself might take up root in his soul if he gives it voice.

There is so much more than friendship between him and the man's wife. He is not in love with her, like a boyhood crush. What he feels for her, what he believes she feels for him, is heaven sent. Perhaps a gift from his own angelic mother, for that is of whom she reminds him. Her gardenia pallor, her melodious voice. The love of his very soul.

"Yes. Rob is off visiting his aunt. Mrs. Stanard…" He shakes the young man's hand as his gaze turns toward the grand stairs.

Edgar has only ascended them once or twice with Rob.

"She is not well enough to receive visitors."

"Yes, sir." Eddy wants to object. "Sir, I've written a poem for the lady. May I give it to her and be off, allow you the evening to yourself?"

Mr. Stanard looks the young man over. He's well dressed, well spoken, a gentlemen in the making, no doubt. "You're the Allan's boy?"

"Yes, sir." He doesn't use the name anymore. Has refused since his adoptive father has not legally made him his very own son. He's heard the rumors of Allan's other children; those his wife couldn't bear, his mistresses have. The man doesn't treat him as his natural borne, doesn't treat his wife as a wife. Allan doesn't deserve the gifts life's given him.

"Ah, yes. Have met the man. Good man."

Eddy half smiles, can't bring himself to agree.

"Well, young man. If you have a poem, I will leave it with my wife. But, as she is indisposed, you'll understand…"

One of the servants rush into the foyer. "Mr. Stanard, sorry to interrupt, but an urgent message has just arrived."

Mr. Stanard barely says good-bye to Edgar as he tells the steward to see him out.

Eddy turns to go, but the servant in his hurried state did not completely close the door. Eddy prods the door open, takes a moment to glance around, then makes for the stairs, lines his body against the wall, surveys up and alternatively down the staircase while he advances to the top.

Trying one door and then another, he watches a nurse leave the sick room. As the nurse makes her way downstairs, Eddy slips into the ill-lit room. Crystal lanterns burn on either side of Mrs. Stanard's bed. Drapes hang around the bedside. The tiny woman glows with sweat and sickness, as waxen as the linens on which she sleeps.

He knows now, Mrs. Stanard will not come back to him, will not hear another of his poems. Never again will he hear the delicious din of her precious praise as he finishes a verse.

He sits in the nurse's bedside chair. Pulling the poem from his pocket, Edgar slides it under her pillow and lingers, staring at her pale face. He's witnessed this before; forever etched on his mind are the beautiful faces of dying women.

Her scarlet lips tremble as she mumbles an incoherent statement. Her hand reaches from under the heavy quilting and rests on top of it. He gingerly lifts his hand. It is improper to touch, he knows. He hesitates but not long before he gently brushes his hand across hers.

He hears, now, in his head, "Do you love me?"

He responds, now, as he might have then, "beyond the shores of my soul."

Her lovely white fingers stretch up, caress his face, tender as the gardenia's petal across his skin.

"Then don't, Eddy, don't." The song starts small and sings out until it becomes a great chorus in his head. The pale petaled fingers becomes thorns that scratch as he tries to pull them away from his face.

His very own hand scrapes at his face, tears the skin. Waking from his death lullaby, he jumps up from his chair at the old wooden desk in his chamber. The small box of a room: bed, dresser, desk. Boston. His home. His betrayer.

"You took them all." He curses the darkness of the space, the stygian void that fills his soul.

He grabs at the vile of liquid on his desk, trips over the chair before he kicks it out of the way and throws himself unceremoniously onto his bed. He sucks another breath from the tiny glass bottle before he crashes it against the window pane.

Noreen Lace

Trees burst forth from the shards of glass and encircle him. It's late-summer, the James River moves leisurely as humidity blankets the city. Edgar pushes his way through the trees, thrusts leaves and branches from his face, ripe dirt spatters his pant legs, his shoes. He's engulfed in blackness once again.

When the obsidian darkness clears, the blaze of the morning sun blinds him. He stands in front of St. John's Church where his own dear mother is buried. He kicks at the sticks and leaves with his feet and twists to listen to the ice crackle on the mulberry tree.

An early frost, then a warm day, the tree shoves off the frozen droplets; the sound is almost musical. He moves closer, allows the chilled beads to fall on his shoulders, observes the harmony of nature as life challenges death.

At his feet, unmarked graves. His beloved mother is among them, but he wonders which one as he unhurriedly paces past them. He pauses where he was brought as a child. An unmarked grave fit for an actress. He hears her voice, but the words are lost within the symphony of nature's song.

Another voice sings out. Different than the melody between life and death, winter and spring. He strolls to the back of the church, certain he hears his name soft and sylphlike floating on the wind. He wanders from the church, through the streets as a mist settles down around the city, toward the murmur until it becomes clear and definitive.

He pauses, somewhere between his and her home, where the haze begins to dissipate. He waits, watches the young woman wave goodbye to her father from the steps of her little candent house.

Eddy waits until the father is out of sight before he reveals himself. She doesn't see him as she turns to go in.

He stands across the dirt road from Elmira's home, tries to assess the movement inside. He crosses the street and knocks on the door.

The housekeeper lets him in. He sits, waits.

"Eddy!" Elmira flies into the room and hugs him. When the housekeeper clears her throat in the hall, Elmira releases his neck, steps away from him.

They sit across from one another. Her hands are folded in her lap as he leans forward toward her with a desire to caress those lily-like fingers. They have held hands, hugged, in secret places, in quiet places; he's even felt her lips like summer buttercups upon his.

He imagines her in the garden where they sometimes meet so as not to be found out. But it's only stolen moments here and there.

"Father just left," she offers shyly.

"I know," he nods.

"He doesn't want me to see you."

"I know that too," he pauses. "But once I'm back from college, once my father assents…" his voice trails off. That's a slim hope. He'll study what his father desires, to live the life everyone expects.

He shakes his head, leans closer to Elmira and takes her hand in his. He'll try. But his passion blooms elsewhere. Only she understands.

The door opens and the young couple jump up. Her father has returned. Eddy's hand is still entwined with her delicate little fingers.

"Mr. Royster." Edgar holds out his hand as gentlemen are expected to do.

"Mr. Allan." Elmira's father ignores the offered handshake.

"Poe," Eddy corrects him. He doesn't intend to be disrespectful, but it's habit now to use his birth name.

"I'd prefer if you not see my daughter when I am not present."

A mist blows the door open, slamming it against the wall. The thick blanched mass sweeps through the room, encloses them all in its grasp, swallows Mr. Royster whole. Eddy holds tight to Elmira's hand. Even as he loses sight of her, she calls to him, "Eddy, Eddy."

She's dragged slowly, slowly away from him until she too succumbs to the haze that surrounds them. Her hand slips from his and he beats his way through the menacing abstract brume.

He rushes in the direction of the door, charges through the thickening cumulus, calls, "El... El...." only to have his voice sucked into the vacuum.

He reaches the door, pulls himself out. Out of the house. Out of the oppressing heather fog.

The sun momentarily blinds him; he raises a hand to shade his eyes. The clouds have given way to a thicket of trees. Somewhere in the center of the garden, she waits for him.

He races through the foliage to a clearing. There's soft, green grass under his bare feet. She waits for him on a makeshift bench of broken stumps.

As he races toward her, Elmira opens her arms again, welcomes him. They cannot be seen alone together and especially not in this embrace, so she loosens her grip sooner than he wishes.

Eddy kisses her slight hand, sits next to her. "As soon as I return from college, my dearest El, no one will keep us apart. I'll set up a little house for us. You'll see, my darling, your father will yield."

Elmira blushes and lowers her head as a shy smile plays on her face. She believes it with her whole heart, if even for a moment.

"Read me a poem, dear Eddy." Her voice is low, overtaken by the birds who play above their heads and the subtle rustling as the wind moves through the leaves of the trees.

He reaches for her chin, raises her face to his before he recites the poem he's prepared. He wants to capture her attention, hold her heart completely.

A shine appears in her eyes, a slight tear stirs in the corner; his poetry evokes warmth throughout her body, an ardor the young girl hasn't experienced before. The flutter in her chest, as if her heart has wings, assures her that Edgar is her destiny.

Eddy sinks in the saturation of the flowers, inhales the scents as the garden overtakes them. The forest plants bloom and grow as night sneaks up on them. Large white flowers blossom at her feet, steal up her legs, and over her body.

Eddy panics, but he's unable to move from the tree stump; the late summer sun has melted his body, melding him with the forest itself. She is the flower, he is the decayed tree on which they sit.

"Eddy," her voice hums through the slight blossoms that bud around her face. "Don't worry, Eddy. We will be together someday."

He reaches for her just as she fades away beyond large colorless blooms.

"But not today, Eddy."

She is gone; the sable forest drops him into lightless obscurity. Trapped. Vines twist around his arms, his legs, his body flat against the ground. Then her voice echoes all around him and vibrates through him.

"Get up, Eddy. Get up, now. Run! Run!"

He flails in the darkness, breaks his arms free, kicks his legs free. He fights back against the blackness, the loneliness that threatens to drag him under.

He jumps up, bloodies his hand against the cold and rusted iron bedframe. Slams his feet, as they hang over the bed, to the wooden floor, again, and again, until he realizes, he is not yet in a shallow grave, but the raven-gloom of the lonely room somewhere in Boston, if his memory serves him.

"Sleep, take me from this nightmare called life," he mumbles as he lays his face into the flat fabric of the pillow. It smells of lye, softened by the aroma of autumn, mixed with the scent of his own sweat.

And then lilacs, somewhere in the heat of the summer sun, the scent of his sweat mixed with the tender blooms of her lilacs.

Her. Lilacs.

And Edgar drifts from obsidian-night to brilliant-day, the dog somewhere out that window, somewhere just beyond his purview, but he can sense the creature, hear the click of his long nails on the brick streets of Philadelphia somewhere behind him, off the main road, he turns, but can't see him.

People bustle about him, his own footsteps echo on the wooden slats of the walkway, then that infernal click-click-click behind him. He steps down, into the roadway and is almost hit by a horse drawn carriage. He jumps out of the way, mud covers his shoes, as he crosses to the other side. He must outrun, out-maneuver that melanoid phantom following him.

He loves Philadelphia, the sights, the movements of people and traffic. The city smells of success, he thinks. He has never felt more alive, more happy than at any time in his life. New buildings, new opportunities, friends, family, he thinks as he advances home.

"Dinner tonight?" His friend calls out to him from the door of Gazette.

"Dinner!" he calls back, quickens his pace. He must reach home. He must get to Virginia, to his writing desk, before tonight.

Then he is home, his little house with a picketed gate and a yard all their own. Their little family, with the woman he now calls Mother, his aunt who has remained true and faithful, who believes in him and has never faltered in her faith in him.

Then her daughter, his wife, his beautiful Virginia. She waits for him at the piano, always at the piano, in her best dress, indigo like her eyes, like her soul. His own one and true love. Her hair is raven-shine and hangs in glistening curls; her pearly skin is dewy in the Philadelphia summer. Her sweet petal like fingers tap the ivory keys. She smiles and his life is complete.

"My dearest Eddy." She reaches out her hand to him. He goes to her, takes her hand, and sits next to her on the piano bench, brushes his skin to hers. He wants to know it's real.

Every day he touches her like this, cheek to cheek, palm in palm, to make certain she is tangible. She is the light in a life fraught with shadows. She chases the caliginous fog away. Hardships taught him to appreciate softness – her. He takes her fingers, cuddles each to his lips. She is the warm summer sun to his chilled life.

"Go, silly, I must practice if I am to entertain our guests tonight."

Eddy backs out of the room. He must finish the poem; the right words, the blithe rhythm has eluded him for days. But he is distracted.

Her hands glide over the keys, the melodic, sweet sounds from her tiny fingers, her unpainted nails tick on the ivory keys, and the sounds illuminate gentle at first and then become round and thick until they fill the room. His desk vibrates, once, twice. He knows it's not her music distracting him; it's the vibrations of someone, no, something else.

As he rises, he turns, believes he sees a form, hears a whimper in the corner. He thinks to chase it away, but their friends have arrived. The night seems to go on forever, they joke and laugh, enjoy dinner at the table, then drinks around the fireplace before the entertainment begins. The rooms are filled with comfort, color, beauty. This is the life he's always wanted.

Eddy reads to his wife and friends, another torrid tale, they say. Then Virginia moves to the piano. She plays one melody, pauses for a sip of water to tamp down a scratch in her throat, then her fingers pound the keys harder than a small hand should seem to, then she stutters and wheezes before beginning the piece again.

Eddy and their friends watch, listen to the music. This is bliss, Eddy thinks just before Virginia's cough becomes unstoppable, before blood spatters the blanched keys and drips from her rosy lip onto the violet dress.

"Eddy?" Her voice is lost in the chaos of the moment.

He grabs a handkerchief and wipes her mouth. "It's nothing, it's nothing." He's lying to himself and, somewhere deep inside, he knows this.

She coughs again and again, first tiny dots of bright red spray the keys, but soon the snowy keys run with crimson, thick puce drops and splotches all about them. She rasps again and the alcove fills with vermilion waters.

He dabs the cloth at her mouth, her hands, the keys. "It is nothing." He watches the rising floodwaters move toward them. "You've practiced too much, my darling. You've played too hard."

He turns to explain to their friends, but they are alone. The brilliance of their living room gone, the sounds of the city lost.

When he turns back to Virginia, they are in a small bedroom, bleak walls, thick blankets. Their former lives gone, Virginia lies asleep, calm and quiet. The cloth still in his hand, the red stain turns to maroon as the barium-orange sun sets in the winter sky.

He sits next to her, "A dream," he sucks in a breath. "It was all a dream." He breathes a sigh of relief as he rubs his hand over his face, tries to wake himself from the nightmare.

Virginia's eyes flutter open. "My dearest Eddy."

His soul quivers back to life. With hope. A tiny ruby dot appears on her chin, another on her cheek, a spot on the pillow next to her.

"It's nothing," he says to himself as he leans closer and touches the points with his fingertip, once fushia, now rust.

She coughs florid splashes of death.

He returns the cloth, dabs her mouth. He repeats, "it's nothing," but he knows he lies.

Virginia chokes; long vines of red blood pour from her lips.

He wrenches at the garnet ropes as they wrap themselves around her petite body. He yanks and tears at them, but they multiply, envelop her as he continues to fight for her. Then, finally, he yells, "Take me, too!" as the rich rouge lianas turn into thick bush. Soon, he can see nothing beyond thorny brush.

Virginia disappears into the carmine nebulous, which dissolves into onyx before his eyes.

He's alone in the shadows once again. There is nothing without Virginia. There are no ideas, no writing, no love, no desire to go on. Hard, bleak, darkness.

The last of her medicine, the last of his tincture is next to the bed in the forest of trees. The last gulp of laudanum promises to end his life. If she dies, he cannot go on. He will not go on.

He reaches his hand from the bed, through the obscurity of the forest for that wooden desk to the tiny bright liquid in the brown pharmacists' bottle. The magical syrup shines, a beacon of hope, the betrayer of life, both of which promise to reunite him with his loves: his own beloved mother, his own dear soul love, his own beautiful wife.

"No, Eddy, no," Virginia whispers through the abyss.

He rasps to the crimson death. "Take me with."

The black dog howls. His knotted and bloodied hand reaches from the grave in which he lies, through the thicket of prickered branches to the brown bottle and, just as he grasps it, the icy raw hand of death clutches his wrist.

He wakes with a start. His addled brain tries to make sense of the ink-like box in which he lies; for certain he's buried in a coffin, but not quite dead. He can feel the frozen dirt from the brisk winter surround him. He shakes off the haze, forces his eyes open.

The flat, somewhere in Boston. The moonlight through the trees throw specters all around him. The branches edge close, the artic ground moves under him. A beam sets the bottle aglow.

"The last gulp will bring me home," he tries to call out, but he can no longer hear his own voice.

More than half way to death's door; he knows it now.

The night howls, the wind hammers at the window, ushering the curtains from the thin frame. The moonlight splashes in, milky, yellow, then cherry, as Eddy grabs for the tincture. He thinks, yes. He thinks, finally.

There's a flash of luminescence; the room fills with warmth, Virginia's laughter bathes his soul, the applause of the audience hushes his pounding head, the heat from his mother's body warms him.

Then it's gone.

But the howling, growling of some not so far off creature remains. There's a rustling, rattling, clicking against the window from some errant bird.

"Stop," he tries to say. "Stop these damned distractions."

For an instant Virginia's in the other room, the piano plays, but then he's here again, the clatter against the window, the howl of the dog, the rays from a magenta moon lull him.

The tincture, he reaches, it's within his grasp, when a soft and dewy hand reaches up between the bed and desk and grasps his within its own tiny fingers. They are ivory, almost bone, but hot, and he is the one who is cold, shivering, near death.

"No, Eddy, no." The whisper slithers around his skull, echoes bounce from wall to wall until the words becomes a scream. "NO EDDY NO!"

Eddy shoves himself from the bed, falls to the floor. He kicks his feet, claws backward until his shoulders slam against the door. He sits, unmoving, with the frozen wood of the door against the back of his head and the chilled wood slats of floor boards beneath him.

Radiance mixes with night, brumes of fog and clouds, branches reach out, and shadows dart as the room swirls, and dips, and curves. Beasts roar from the aphotic corners, screams dive at him, glass cracks and shatters.

He's sinking. Certain he's dead. The clank of chains and the squeals of a pulley lower him into a frigid grave.

He forces his hands over his ears to block out the horror.

"I surrender," he screams.

The room drops into stilled silence.

He dares try his eyes, removes his hands from his ears. He's still against the door, on the floor; his body is slow to obey, as if he's moving through quicksand. He pushes to his knees, crawls across the floor to the chair, the desk, hoists himself ever so deliberately up.

He leans over the desk, toward the window, head bleating, heart pounding, legs shaking. He's half dressed, the torn and untucked clothing hangs from his frame. He's chilled, sore, and sick.

His knotted hands are covered in dried blood he thinks, but then notices the ink spilled across the desk. He splays out his fingers, something still in his hand, lifts his palm to his face.

The last drops of the poison that might've taken him shimmy in the bottle. Feeling the torturous night throughout his soul and angry at his own mortality and immortality, he raises the bottle far above his head and crashes it against the wall where the glass shatters and the liquid splatters.

Stars play in the azure sky as the first rays of morning light streak across the horizon. He lowers his heavy body into the chair. He retrieves paper from the desk drawer, uprights the half empty ink jar, reaches for the old quill pen. There is only one purpose now. Only one.

The End

Author's note:

Like many, I came across Edgar Allan Poe when I was quite young, probably, through his famous poem, *The Raven*. It wasn't until years later I understood and could articulate the full importance of Poe and his work.

In the early 1800's, our leaders called for our writers to create a truly American Literature, different and unique from British Literature, to individualize ourselves from the motherland.

Poe differentiated himself from many authors of the time and created stories that horrified and intrigued readers. He is the original creator and, therefore, the grandfather of our modern horror, psychological thriller, mystery, and detective fiction. He succeeded in producing an exceptional and lasting impression of American literature, which has continued to inspire.

Beyond what many people know, Edgar Allan Poe was also an essayist. He wrote about street paving, Stonehenge, and he analyzed the fraud of tricksters. Finally, he was a true literary critic. Not only had he his own thoughts and beliefs about what made good literature, he did deep analyses of other's writings and offered honest opinions. This did not win him friends; his purpose was (most likely) to design what he believed were valuable tools with which to read and write literature.

Poe was much more than *The Raven*. He was much more than a near dead, desaturated image on copperplate. Paintings done a year or two prior to his suicide attempt show a healthy, handsome man, one who was thriving in his life and his community.

Maybe the reasons we love Poe so much, even today, is that Americans sympathize with the orphan, empathize with and relate to the underdog. He struggled most of his life and, through the hardship and pain, he created a legacy of literary art which has lasted far beyond his time and will continue far beyond ours.

Noreen Lace received an MFA from California State University, where she now teaches. She believes in the beauty of language to express the darkness in life. She is the author of two novellas, West End and Life of Clouds, as well as two books of short stories, Here in the Silence and Namas-Cray.

Her fiction and poetry have appeared in national as well as international journals, including The Chicago Tribune's Printers Row Journal, The Oleander Review, Vine Leaves Press, Wild Woman Medicine Circle, Pilcrow and Dagger, and others. "Memorial Day Death Watch," a memoir of her father's passing, placed as a finalist in Writer Advice while her poem, "All at Once," was published as a finalist in Medusa's Laugh Contest issue.

Edgar Allan Poe remains a passion as she teaches, lectures, and was interviewed on Super News Live's show Dark Times about Poe's influential life and mysterious death.

www.NoreenLace.com

Also by Noreen Lace

West End
Life of Clouds
Here in the Silence
Namas-Cray